Chicken 'n Dumplins 'n Death
A Columbia River Gorge Mystery
by A. Zed

CHICKEN 'N DUMPLINS 'N DEATH

First edition. April 21, 2021.

Copyright © 2021 A. Zed.

ISBN: 979-8201637972

Written by A. Zed.

Table of Contents

The map.

A diagram of major locations on the bus tour.

The disclaimer.

This is a work of fiction. Sassy, saucy fiction. All characters and places are the product of the author's vivid imagination or are used fictitiously with a healthy serving of creative license. All restaurants, parks departments, and waterfalls involved are unwitting, innocent participants in this fictional drama.

The dedication.

This story is dedicated to Jonny, my love dumpling.

The story.

The gravy thickens.

In the moments before one of my tripmates planted face down in a plate of dumplings, I had been thinking what a successful trip it had been. I already had what I came for: maybe a dozen excellent photographs of Columbia River Gorge scenery (along with a few hundred mediocre ones). And happy memories of quality time with one of my best friends, Sue. That, too.

But what I'm saying is that I'd already gotten what I wanted out of the trip. I was content. It would've been fine by me to skip Tad's Chicken 'n Dumplins Roadhouse Diner altogether.

And given what occurred there, I suspect the deceased man would have agreed with that plan.

Not that Sue would have let me skip the Chicken 'n Dumplins stop of the field trip. I mean, she would have if she'd known someone would die there, of course. Before she retired, Sue had been a nurse after all, a professional at saving lives. Not sitting around watching people succumb to violent death.

But there we were, eating our dumplings under a cloud of doom because none of us had imagined that an innocent dinner could end up like that.

Well, one of us had imagined it, I guess.

But the person responsible for that particular course of events sure hadn't factored in me being there, ready to stop them from getting away with it.

Oh yeah.

For those of you who don't know me, I'm Bertha May Olson. Two hundred and sixteen pounds of fun. I used to go by Beth, and even Betty for a while. Back when I was trying to be the slim person I was never born to be. But after the kids and foster kids and everything else, I gave up on those attempts to be someone I wasn't. I leaned in, as they say these days. Instead of trying to follow the fashions (and never keeping up), I let my beautician give me a nice big perm, I tossed out everything from my closet but muumuus and stretch pants and sweatshirts, and I got comfortable just being me. My horn-rim glasses aren't trendy vintage. They're just old. Like me. And I'm ok with that.

The funny thing is how I've been able to use this – how quick folks are to overlook the hefty lady in the wheelchair and say or do things they wouldn't in front of someone they thought was worth impressing. I'm not afraid to say it: I'm smarter than most, but no one seems to assume that when they first meet me. Funny how, in the end, people's prejudices end up biting them in the butt.

I'm a retired civil servant living in a nursing home in central Kansas. And yes, as you probably know, my friends back home and I have developed a bit of a reputation for solving mysteries. Which comes in handy more often than we'd like. But I was expecting a little break from all that when I went on vacation to visit my dear old friend Sue in Portland, Oregon.

Sue made all the plans to join the van tour with her local parks department. She's a peach and never complains about the places I drag her when she visits me, so I had to return the favor and roll with it.

Well, I *might* have done a little complaining. All in good fun.

"So you think I need more dumplings in me, Sue?" I'd asked her while we were planning the trip.

"It's an historic experience, Bertha May," she'd coaxed me. "Tad's has been a part of Columbia River Gorge for nearly a century. It's part of history."

"Historic dumplings, you say? I prefer mine fresh, thank you."

It was true that I of all people did not need more dumplings in my life or in my belly, between the diabetes and arthritis and whatever new diagnoses the doctors were always coming up with for me. My weekly pillbox was no joke.

I could hardly believe that a parks department had organized a whole tour to help senior citizens eat dumplings, but Sue said that was only half of it. The van trip tootled along the Columbia River Gorge, a prized jewel of the Pacific Northwest. The natural history justified indulging in the greasy food, I suppose. And the scenery was what sold me – not that I don't love a good plate of chicken, mind you, just not so much I'd spend all day in a cramped van with strangers to eat it.

So the day trip was Sue's idea. Thanks to her dragging me along, I got photos, more dumplings than I ever needed, and the chance to catch a killer. I can blame – I mean, thank – Sue for that.

Call it *The Case of Tad's Dumplings*.

No, no, *A Tad Too Much Chicken Murder*.

No, *Case of the* –

Whatever. A man was dead, face down on the dinner table at Tad's historic roadside diner at the end of an eventful day.

Sue. Me.

Sue, I should say, is short for Susan Hummel, retired RN and now full-time volunteer. She's been my friend for years, since our college days. She went on to become a nurse, moved out to Oregon, and now that she's retired, she's throwing her energetic little self full-time into advocacy for public health and seniors and the disabled. She sits on various community boards and whatnot. Stays busy.

She's short but slim, pale, with long, straight white hair she wears pinned back in a neat pony tail. Always tidily dressed. Her face can look stern at first, until you get it to break into a mischievous, almost elfin smile. She's a handsome lady, if you ask me. And I won't lie to you that she's got some quirks. Her handwashing, for one thing: too much time in hospitals and reading about public health, I guess. She knows too much.

All of which might make you wonder what she was doing trying to talk her diabetic friend into going on a road trip to a dumpling restaurant. I knew something was up. And the answer to that, I quickly found out, rested in the leadership of these trips for seniors by Portland Parks & Rec.

Specifically, one tall, handsome leader, by the name of Quaid Moorhouse.

Sue had started going on some of these van trips for the 60-plus set over the past years. Only lately had she gotten so excited about them, after a trip to a lantern show at Fort Vancouver last month. That's where she started swooning over this Quaid character. She gushed that he was a vivacious leader, that he always had fun surprises for each group. I knew there was more she wasn't telling me, or maybe even herself.

Now I would have the chance to meet the fellow Sue kept mentioning. Get a look at him myself. Not that she came out and said she was sweet on him.

"I can't wait to meet your crush, Sue," I had told her that morning.

"Don't be silly, Bertha May. A 'crush?' I'm not a teenager!"

But she was behaving just the way I'd seen enough times over the years. I'd been her college roommate, after all. Even though it had been a few decades and marriages since then, I knew what I was seeing. Quiet, gentle Sue, just happening to mention a certain fellow a little more frequently than usual. Just a little more excited about the van trip than it warranted. Just a little more time spent grooming herself at the mirror before we set out that morning. A few little clues, but enough.

I'm observant like that.

How it began.

The day started with the group of us meeting up at the East Portland Community Center, hovering awkwardly, making chitchat, until the van pulled up and we piled in.

"All aboard the Elderwagon," joked one of our tripmates, Lou, as the van arrived. The name stuck.

Sue had checked ahead of time, and sure enough, the van accommodated my motor scooter. Which impressed me – this Portland Parks & Rec was ahead of the curve on that front. So I zoomed in, got my chair strapped down, Sue claiming a seat nearby, and we settled in for the ride to our first stop at one of the Gorge's gorgeous waterfalls.

Before we get to that, though, let me lay out for you who else was on the trip.

There were ten of us participants in total. Sue and me, of course.

There was Olaf, a friendly fellow with a walker, in a Nordic print red-and-gray sweater. Olaf seemed to be just a quiet, jolly good sport, laughing along with everyone chatting around him. Then on the quiet parts of the ride, I realized he was laughing to himself just as much as before. He laughed every few minutes, no matter what was going on around him. Ah well, he was having a good time, and who was that hurting?

I wasn't the only one on a motor scooter. Always nice to have company. A woman named Thuy was on wheels like me, dropped off at the van by her daughter. Thuy had to be pushing ninety. When we did get a word with her, between her catnaps on the bus, she seemed nice enough. And my word, she was a speed demon. She pushed her scooter to the limits, even loading onto the van. That machine seemed to have two settings, under her control: stopped or full-speed ahead.

Next there was Joyce. She was there with her caregiver, Astana, who was a slightly bored-looking Ukrainian woman who talked very loudly and severely on the occasions when she did speak. From what I could tell, Joyce wasn't hard of hearing, but Astana apparently had only one, loud volume for clients. Joyce was maybe in her young sixties, slim, highly mobile. In fact, I couldn't perceive any physical disability about her, which clued me in right away to her having one of the many disabilities that aren't visible but serious enough to get to the point of requiring a caregiver. There are more people like that than folks realize, partly because society does such a bad job of including them. Joyce seemed a little nervous, but it's always hard to tell when you just meet someone what they're usually like. Whatever she was living with, it really didn't matter. She was along for the ride, pleasant to talk to, and it wasn't my business to ask any questions I wouldn't be interested in answering about myself.

The remaining four members of the group were two married couples, Marsha and Milton, and Charlene and Lou. As I came to learn from our brief introductions waiting in the parking lot, and then from overhearing their loud conversation from the back of the van, the two couples were neighbors at their retirement center.

Marsha was a retired schoolteacher and Milton was a retired accountant (they both looked the parts). They'd raised their family in Portland.

Lou and Charlene were more recent transplants to the city. He had been a farmer in Eastern Oregon, one of the few who'd made that career lucrative. Lou was the wise-guy who nicknamed our van the "Elderwagon." You could tell upon first meeting that Lou was a guy used to working a room. Charismatic, handsome. His wife Charlene, made up immaculately, hung on his arm.

Marsha and Milton were taking the trip to celebrate their 42nd wedding anniversary. And their friends Charlene and Lou were also celebrating an anniversary, the coming month, but for only two years of marriage.

Two years, you wonder?

Look, life is tough. Lots happens. Don't let me of all people sound judgmental of others' life choices. Old folks like us should be the most tolerant of anyone: we've seen it all and done most of it ourselves. Live and let live.

But I'd also learned over the years that there were only a few scenarios by which a nice older couple like that ended up married for two years. Some were heart-warming; others were head-shaking. And judging solely by the tone of what was said and unsaid, I was guessing I knew which one it was.

Earthly beauty.

Just getting onto the Elderwagon, I could tell what had gotten Sue all twitterpated. By the looks of it, Sue had good taste.

In addition to the van driver and a young park ranger who spent most of the ride with earbuds in, there was this Quaid Moorhouse fellow, the "Adult Activity Coordinator," according to his badge. He was a definite draw. Tall, strong, handsome in the nice grizzled way that men only come into in their sixties. A rich, warm smile through his grey beard. With sunglasses, a wide-brimmed hat, and a funky floral-print button-up shirt, he literally wore his charm and spunk on his sleeve. He emanated a fun, light spirit. In my stretched-out sweats and fleece jacket, I was clearly underdressed for the festive occasion Quaid had shown up for.

Our van cruised eastward down Interstate-84 to our first stop, at Horsetail Falls. As we rode along, Sue hardly seemed to notice the scenery – outside the Elderwagon, that is.

Meanwhile, I was enjoying it all. Not just the fun of watching Sue swoon but also the actual purpose of the trip: to see "the Gorge," as locals call it.

I had driven along the Columbia River Gorge before, but it had been years. It's truly a glorious corner of creation. Eons ago, a huge ice dam broke out in Montana, and released a cascade of water that flooded down to the Pacific Ocean, all that water carrying rocks and ice and other chunky stuff that carved out the steep banks of the Gorge, creating the pathway for the Columbia River to flow into the sea. The Columbia starts up in Canada, but down here where it forms the border between Oregon and Washington, its banks are the result of those prehistoric Missoula Floods.

The Gorge cuts a path right through the Cascade Mountains – that string of volcanic peaks you've heard of, like Mt. Hood and Mt. St. Helens. The result is a stunning scene, with stark cliffs cutting down steep toward the wide river. On the west side of the mountains, toward the ocean, the land stays wet and green pretty much year-round. The other, eastern side of the mountains is another story: dry and brown. But this van tour stayed on the green, lush side, where streams make dramatic leaps down the cliff faces to form a series of scenic waterfalls. Horsetail Falls didn't fail to delight.

As I've mentioned, I was on this ride for the vistas – the waterfalls, river, valleys, mossy glens, lush green forests unlike anything we've got back home. I've got a decent little camera, and I'm not too humble to say that I've also got an eye for nice shots.

I'm observant, and that applies in multiple arenas. Photography is the nice way. Less pleasantly, it applies when I'm catching murderers and thieves and arsonists who think they can pull a fast one on an old lady like me. But when they do, I tell ya, they find out quick that my mind moves even faster than my motor scooter.

Girl talk.

"*Girl talk?*"

Gag me. That's not what I call it. I'm not a *girl*. Haven't been for a good long time.

But that's what two members of our trip were gushing about as they pushed into the women's restroom.

"So nice to get a minute for some girl talk!" Charlene giggled to Marsha.

We were at Multnomah Falls, the crown jewel of the Gorge waterfalls, a towering cliff face with a braid of water descending over 600 feet. I'd already taken in the falls and cruised through the small room with displays about natural history. Only so much you need to learn about the life stages of fish. I was parked in the (thankfully accessible) restroom, waiting for the handicapped stall to open up. Someone had been in there quite a while, but patience is one of the skills I've been forced to develop, being me. And, like many other of my skills, it comes in handy at odd times.

Thanks to me having to sit there, and thanks to them seemingly ignoring my existence completely, I got to overhear the entire conversation between Marsha and Charlene when they paraded through the restroom. Amazing what people will talk about in public. Public restrooms, anyway.

Of course, not knowing these women from Eve, I couldn't tell if they were the sort of people who talked about money like this in front of just anyone. Or just a nobody in a motor scooter.

The topic of the day was Lou's new will. Which, to Charlene's obvious delight, he had just rewritten, to include her receiving a third of his estate, the same as each of his two kids.

"It's just beautiful how much he loves me," Charlene was gushing. "I mean, being in his will – that's true love."

"Oh, that's nice." I wasn't sure that Marsha agreed, but she was trying to be polite. "How do his kids feel about that?"

"Oh, you know, they're mad, of course. But it's not like there isn't plenty to go around! Lou is real smart with money. He even helped out the other farmers around him, loaned them money when they were broke, that sort of thing. It's such a shame he couldn't stay in business out there, he loved it so."

Marsha said, "A pity."

Charlene huffed, "His kids just want our money. I mean, they hardly ever call, they only visit when Lou's in the hospital. They've been nothing but rude to me. They don't even put my name on cards when they write to Lou."

"They're still mad about the divorce?"

"I suppose that's it. They blame me for it all. But Lou wasn't happy with Felicia for years. Those kids just take their mother's side of everything. How can they blame us for wanting to be happy?"

The two women were fixing up their makeup, their purses planted on the counter by the pair of sinks. Apparently, they had not believed the announcement by the park ranger that their possessions would be safe and sound in the van with the driver. Or maybe they just needed their beauty supplies with them wherever they went. *Girls will be girls...*

"Where is Felicia these days?"

"Back in Pendleton, still. She got the town – pretty much ran Lou out. You'd think that would be enough. Poor Lou had to give up his whole business – sell everything he'd worked for! It was too small of a town for all three of us, running into each other at the grocery store and church. We had to move out here, to get some space. Get a new start."

By that point, the women were on their way out the door, having not acknowledged my existence apart from an awkward smile from Marsha. And I was still waiting for the accessible stall to open up. With increasingly less patience.

Fortunately, the next people to come in were Joyce and her caregiver, Astana. Seeing me waiting, they checked and found out that it hadn't just been an incredibly shy, quiet potty user in there, but that the stall was empty and just jammed shut. Astana, clearly experienced at this sort of thing, used a comb to finagle the stall lock and then shoved the door open for me. My savior!

Back on the van, I found out I wasn't the only one grateful Astana had come on the trip. The young park ranger, by the name of Rick, had taken out his earbuds and opened his eyes. As soon as Astana returned to the van, he was leaning back across the seats, trying to get the pretty Slavic caregiver talking. It was natural enough – and I couldn't fault him for his taste. Ranger Rick seemed nerdy, but sincere. Astana was a looker. She was older than him and way out of his league, I wagered, but there was no harm in a little flirtation for a day.

That seemed to be Sue's logic with her crush on Quaid. Which made ample entertainment for me: watching my old friend behaving like those twenty-somethings.

The romance of falling.

After Multnomah Falls, we stopped at Wahkeena Falls, just a short ways along the Columbia River Historic Highway we were taking back toward Portland. We were making our way west along the slow historic route, having looped past the whole series of falls on Interstate 84 at the start of the day.

"This next one's a '7,'" I heard a voice chirp from the back of the van. "Ooh, and it has a *kissing bridge!*"

I knew right then that it was Charlene. She'd picked up a book from the gift shop at Multnomah Falls that offered hiking suggestions themed around 'outdoor romance,' whatever that means. And she'd been unable to resist telling us all about her purchase, as we piled into the van. It *was* her and Lou's anniversary next month, after all, and maybe they would come back for some more intimate hikes.

Which was not something I felt like envisioning.

"What's a kissing bridge?" Marsha asked. Maybe she hadn't been swept away by the romance of her own anniversary trip.

"Ask Milton to help you find out," Charlene giggled.

I glanced back quickly to see the poor husband blushing beet red.

Charlene was undeterred. "Wahkeena Falls is ranked a 7 for romance. The recommended kissing spots are a wooden footbridge and a stone bridge with an archway." She read aloud, "'A kiss in the mist at the bridge is a must!' Doesn't that sound lovely, honey?"

"Mmm hmm," Lou murmured, clearly less excited by 'outdoor romance' than his bride. Or maybe just uninterested in publicly discussing make-out spots.

I decided to chime in. "But how accessible is it for wheelchairs? That's what I want to know. Is it a 7?"

My friend Sue felt the need to reassure me about this. And I really didn't want to sound like a complainer.

Meanwhile, Charlene flipped to another page in her book. "It says the difficulty is a 3... 'Falls visible from parking lot and marginally accessible path.'"

"'Marginally accessible.' I'll take it," I said, wanting to be a good sport for Sue's sake.

Maybe I was just imagining things, but it seemed like Sue was listening rather intently to Charlene reading aloud that book of hers.

Sure enough, the falls proved both accessible and, I suppose, romantic. One cascade pours down behind another, creating a stair-step effect. The roiling white water zig zags through lush foliage coating the rounded rocks on either side. Thick green moss, rolling hills, and trees taller than any I'd seen back home in Kansas. It felt like a land of fairy tales, where forest sprites should appear behind any boulder.

My wheelchair and I did not make it to the designated "kissing spot" on the bridge over the stream, reached only by following a narrow dirt path. And I chose to avert my eyes when I saw Charlene and Lou approaching the stone bridge. I already knew more about their relationship than I'd care to.

However, I did look up and smile when a certain petite white-haired lady stepped onto the bridge, off in the distance from where I was stationed on the trail. Sue had asked me if I'd mind if she ran off down the path to get a closer look. I didn't. I'd learned not to begrudge my more able-bodied friends when they felt the need to use those legs of theirs, legs that for the time being were more helpful than my own; I knew that ability didn't last forever.

I especially didn't mind because I'd seen a certain strapping white-haired gentleman heading up the trail just ahead of Sue. Sure enough, against the backdrop of misting waters, framed by ferns and fir trees, there was my old friend crossing the scenic stone bridge, and there was Quaid, turning around toward her with a smile.

Ok, maybe the author of that romantic hiking guide had a point.

Falling water.

*I*n which Astana saves the day, again.

After Wahkeena, we visited the park at Bridal Veil Falls. That stop was actually designed for those of us on wheels. While others went up a dirt trail or visited the facilities, I cruised around the nice asphalt loop from the parking lot through woods, with some views looking out across the Columbia River to the Washington side. Cars, boats, trains – a whole lotta life flowed back and forth along that Gorge. I met up with Sue later, who'd been hanging around the Elderwagon, I suspected to wait for our esteemed leader/trip heartthrob Quaid.

And after Bridal Veil, we stopped at Shepperd's Dell, but don't ask me much about that one. At some point the waterfalls all started rolling together in my mind. Lordy, that Gorge has a lot of 'em. I mean, they're all beautiful, at least from what I could see from the accessible parts of the trail. For being a handicapped-accessible van trip, this field trip sure had a lot of stops. Off the van, on the van, off the van, on the van. I was just about ready to skip the next one on our tour and stay on the van, but Sue told me it was our last waterfall so I had to see it.

At Latourell Falls, there's a pathway leading all the way down to the base of the falls. You scoot in there (or walk, if you don't have a wheelchair) and you're showered with spray from the water hitting the rocks below. All the rock is black – basalt from prehistoric lava flows, our park ranger, Rick, told us. The black rock is covered in cream-colored lichen and lime green mosses. It's as beautiful as Sue promised. With a huge waterfall just down a short trail, I was astounded that there weren't more people out to see it. The place must be packed on weekends.

The trail was pretty flat, apart from a few lumpy tree roots underneath. But the path was a lot narrower than I was comfortable with. It was tricky to negotiate all the turns, with only a few inches to spare. Olaf, on his walker, had the slowest go of it. Thuy, on the other hand, is a racer. She just shot down the trail on her motorized wheelchair, no looking back. As the nimbler members of the trip went on ahead, I was more cautious – I had no interest in ending up down a muddy cliff, thank you very much.

When we got up to the base of the falls, Thuy was chatting in Vietnamese with a family – the only other visitors on the trail. Charlene and Marsha were posing together for a selfie, squinting up at Charlene's phone camera, while the falls sprayed their poofs of hair. As we approached, the two wives were waving their husbands over to pose with them. I heard Lou saying to Milton, "Not now. We can talk about it later."

Sue and I took some photos of ourselves with the spray as a backdrop. It was the thing to do.

I started wondering how I'd pull off the seventeen-point turn that might be needed to get my scooter turned around on the narrow path. The sidewalk had a steep, fern-covered hillside on one side, and on the other, an immediate drop-off to the stream beneath the falls. Treacherous. Before I figured it out, though, I noticed Olaf had walked past us, past Thuy and the couples, and almost to the base of the falls. Down where the asphalt gets really slick from the spray.

I watched as Olaf continued pushing on his walker, the path getting slicker by the yard. Then, in slow motion, Olaf kept moving – but not along the path. Hands still gripping the walker, his upper body veered off toward the stream side of the path. Sensing the danger, he'd planted his feet. But his walker was already slipping sideways – along with his hands still tightly gripped to it.

I yelled out, helpless to do more.

Just in time, Joyce's caregiver Astana leapt over to him and grabbed him from the edge. The park ranger joined her in pulling Olaf toward steadier ground.

Watching Astana and Ranger Rick help Olaf made me realize that Astana's official charge, Joyce, was nowhere to be seen.

Stop, before you break my heart.

Back on the van, I noticed our entire company was reassembled, including Joyce. Good news, it seemed. Maybe I'd imagined her being missing at the last stop. Maybe.

Ranger Rick started describing our next stop: a bluff called Vista Point. There's a neat art-deco stained glass roundhouse on a pier jutting out over a cliff. It looks down over the Columbia River, with beautiful views from west to east. The Vista House itself had only a rickety looking plywood ramp to get wheelchairs up and I didn't want to risk it. Thuy was half my size, and always a daredevil, so she didn't think twice about zooming on up. But I decided to stick to fresh air and the views from the sidewalk wrapping around the building. When Joyce came out after just a few minutes, complaining about the tiny print on the historical displays, I knew I'd made the right choice. I didn't need that headache.

At the edge of the cliff, thick cement fencing kept us visitors from plummeting and splattering on the road below, as it twists back and forth around the bluff. I got a few shots of the river framed by the posts, built back in the 1920s and 30s when this highway was first built, steeped in the signature style of that era. Classic, classy.

Sue leaned against the fence as I pulled myself up and leaned out to do the same. Great shots. Took some profiles of Sue, as well, her smooth skin and tidy little features standing out against the puffy white clouds and blue sky.

We chatted a bit about the trip so far. I couldn't help teasing her about flirting with Quaid Moorhouse.

"I'm not flirting, I'm just having a conversation with him. He's such a knowledgeable guide, especially about the rural parts of the state. He's a lifelong Oregonian, a rare breed these days. I've been learning a lot."

Sure you have, I thought but didn't say.

"We're lucky he was able to come today. I guess he wasn't originally scheduled to lead the trip. I heard him talking to the park ranger about that. Really lucky he's the one they got to come along."

"Lucky you didn't drag us onto this trip for nothing, that is."

Sue glared at me.

I asked, "Did he give you any sense about what time we're getting to the restaurant, after all these stops?"

"Were you not enjoying the falls?"

I gritted my teeth and tried to find a way to be polite about it. "Don't get me wrong. I love it here, and the views are great. It's just a little more coming and going than I'm used to. I'm just tired."

"It *is* a lot of stops. But to answer your question, no, Quaid didn't tell me what time we get to Tad's. He did give me a sneak preview of a little surprise he has for the group there, though." Sue had that mischievous smile of hers back on. "I think you'll be amused."

I was wary. "What is it?"

"I think you'll enjoy it better as a surprise." I just had to anticipate Quaid's "surprise" ahead.

There was still ten more minutes until it was time to pile back into the Elderwagon and head out, but I decided to load up early. I was hungry and the sooner I was on board, the quicker everyone could leave.

The van driver was a friendly guy named Eduardo who had recently moved to Oregon from El Salvador. He was standing by the van, out to stretch his legs, but he let me on. That was how I discovered what Joyce was up to when she wasn't on the trails with the group: back in her seat on the van, even earlier than me.

So that's where she's been.

"Oh!" she said, upon seeing me enter.

"Hello," I replied.

Joyce looked uncomfortable, but honestly, that wasn't so unusual for her. She smiled at me, then said, "I was just sitting quietly in here. All the crowds... kind of get me nervous. And I've gotten a terrible headache..."

I could respect that. "I understand completely. I won't bother you with talking. I'm just resting up, myself."

Joyce looked grateful, then leaned her head back against the headrest, eyes shut, and fingers to her temples. She started breathing very purposefully.

That's some serious social anxiety, I thought to myself. As I watched the river out the window, I said a silent prayer for the lady.

A tad too much chicken.

Finally, the part you've been waiting for. We arrived at Tad's Chicken 'n Dumplins Roadhouse Diner, where one of our fellow voyagers met his maker in a plate full of gravy and dumplings.

The diner of death.

First, allow me to explain a few events leading up to that point. Such as Chicken Man.

I should start by telling you about Tad's itself. Tad's Diner is "historic" in that it's old. The original was built right along the Columbia River Highway when the road was first opened in 1922. Then in the 40s, Tad's moved to its current location. It was a prime spot for travelers along the historic route that was a gem of the pre-Eisenhower road system. However, once Interstate-84 was built, the number of folks traveling along the original highway plummeted: who chooses the windy twists and turns when you could be going 75 mph?

Tad's, however, wasn't about to move a second time. The place sits right off a narrow parking strip along the old highway, almost falling off the hillside into one of the tributaries to the Columbia. It's nestled amongst tall, mossy trees, so it feels more pleasant than "roadside dining" might convey. Its back end juts out toward the sweet little Sandy river, and half the tables have views through big windows. A porch looks out over the water.

Unfortunately, the group room they reserved for us did not have river views. A nice big window, but facing parallel to the river and highway, so all we were looking out at were big green trees. Not bad on its own, except for knowing that other people were looking out the window at a river.

The interior décor of the place was woodsy. Honey-colored wood paneling, a dark wood bar. Several framed black-and-white photos from the "historic" era of the place were hung on every free inch of wall space.

Well, we got ourselves into the side room reserved for our group, and everyone got themselves situated. Lou, Charlene, Milton, and Marsha took the spots at the far end of the big table, by the window. Thuy and I each picked a side of the table to roll our chairs up to, then Sue planted herself by me while Olaf and Joyce sat next to Thuy. Joyce's caregiver sat next to her, of course, which prompted Ranger Rick to sit next to her, as he'd been angling for her attention ever since Multnomah Falls. Couldn't blame them – the only two people under the age of 40 on the trip, they were bound to have more to say to each other than to us. All that left Quaid sitting at the end of the table right next to Sue, which pleased her just fine.

We pored over the menus and ordered, though Charlene was fretting so much about what to get that she made the waitress come back and take her order last. She ended up just telling Lou to pick something for her. Marsha looked slightly exasperated by her friend's ineptitude, and I could agree with that. I have no patience for women hamming up their role as the "weaker sex" and depending on men.

Nothing else to report about that part of the meal, except that I was a little surprised when Thuy ordered a martini. My kind of lady.

Just as we got our orders in and I thought we would finally have a few minutes to rest, Quaid left the room with a wink at Sue. She just blushed like a schoolgirl. Apparently, she'd been cued, so she awaited her moment to perform.

After a few moments of chitchat, Sue addressed the table of us. "Quaid wanted me to let you know that we are expecting a special visitor to join us."

In answer to the confused looks on faces all around, a large chicken entered the room.

A six-and-a-half-foot tall chicken, clucking and squawking.

I had no idea what to make of it. I had to assume this was the surprise Quaid had told Sue about. A visit from Chicken Man just before we eat chicken. Hilarious?

I'm not sure what effect Quaid was hoping to have with his chicken costume – whether he thought we'd all be laughing like a group of preschoolers at these antics. But no one was as amused as he might have hoped. The man-bird squawked louder, to little effect. Marsha and Milton smiled politely. I noticed Ranger Rick mouth to Astana, "All Quaid's idea, not me." The only one laughing at the chicken was Olaf, but Olaf laughed at most anything.

We were all a little relieved when Sue made another announcement. Apparently, the chicken couldn't talk, or so the schtick went. She said that Quaid the Chicken was inviting us to take a group photo on the porch overlooking the river. Great idea, but it entailed hauling ourselves across the whole restaurant. Which meant me backing my scooter out and Olaf struggling out of his chair to keep up with the more limber trip members. Thuy of course had shot across the restaurant first.

We crossed the room between tables to the wide wooden porch overlooking the river. It was, I had to admit, a beautiful backdrop. A wooden bench for Joyce and Marsha and Olaf to sit on, with me and Thuy on either side, and the rest of the group behind us. Chicken Man stood in the middle of the row behind the bench, his wings up in some sort of avian victory celebration.

Our waitress dutifully snapped our picture for us on my camera. I remember that photo clearly, because I ended up looking at it quite a few times.

Dumplings of doom.

As we made our way back inside, I noticed Milton trying to keep Lou back, to talk to him about something, but just then Charlene tugged on her spouse's arm.

"No business today, boys," I heard Charlene say as she coaxed Lou toward the far end of the porch. "I found another of those 'kissing spots,' honey."

Back inside the diner, we returned to our seats and Chicken Man departed. A few minutes later, Quaid Moorhouse reappeared.

I had to wonder how many kids' parties that routine had actually worked for. Did Quaid play Santa Claus as well?

He looked rather pleased with himself, oblivious to our lack of enthusiasm for his antics. I remembered Sue saying he had a "surprise" for every group he led. Were any of them more entertaining?

"Sorry to be gone, folks. What did I miss?" he asked, with a twinkle in his eye. Sue was the only one who laughed. I hoped Sue didn't see my eyes rolling.

When soup bowls arrived at our tables, everyone tucked in. Most of us were eating silently, but the two married couples at the end of the table carried on their conversation, as they had through most of the trip. Their mealtime discussion was one familiar to each of us older folks.

The pill routine.

As the meals appeared, so did the pill boxes. Astana had gotten out Joyce's, and I'd taken mine. Charlene pulled out from her purse the two pill boxes for herself and Lou, each one the four-by-seven variety with a cubby for each of three meals plus bedtime, for a week. We also got to hear about Marsha and Milton's smaller pill boxes, with only a single compartment for each day of the week, mostly vitamins and thus less time-sensitive.

Any young folks hearing this might be depressed about it, but this is life for us geezers. The huge pillboxes that look so intimidating to you are a huge relief for us old fogeys, because it means we don't have to remember if we took our regular pill already that day or not. Don't have to remember much, in fact. Once a week, we think about our pill schedules, pop the right ones in for each day, and we're set. If there's an empty spot in the pill box for whatever meal we're on, we can rest easy that we're on track.

"Oh, you're lucky you only take vitamins," Charlene said to Marsha. "Look at these huge things we've got! I put our initials on the sides so I don't mix them up. Now, where are we..."

I glanced down the table. Charlene was staring down at the two boxes, her reading glasses perched on the tip of her nose. She was squinting and looking back and forth, running a finger over the days of the week to Friday and down the compartments to the second spot. She popped out the set of pills and started to hand them to her husband.

Marsha put a gentle hand on her arm. "Those are from the box with a 'C' on it. Aren't those yours?"

Charlene froze, a look of embarrassment, then covered it with a chuckle. She set her pills down on her spoon and quickly pulled some out for Lou. Correctly distributed, they each washed their pills down with water, and turned their attention back to their conversation.

Everyone was on top of their pills, it seemed, as the plates of chicken and dumplings were placed before us, family-style, centered nicely at points easily reached by all of us. The dumplings were warm and flakey and savory. Despite everything else that happened, I cannot forget that they were, in fact, delicious.

But then, just as I bit into my second helping of the salty, buttery wonder, the unthinkable happened.

Lou seized up. His face was red and sweaty. He clutched his neck, scratching at his chest. His eyes were bulging. His back spasmed. He looked around the table, at Charlene, at Milton. Then he keeled right over. Right onto his plate of dumplings.

Lou was dead.

The sweet taste of death.

Charlene was screaming, as was Marsha. Milton was panicking, looking around the room. Rick and Quaid and Astana had leapt to their feet, as would I have if I could have. It was so sudden and unnerving, no one wanted to be near whatever was happening to poor Lou, but they also couldn't turn away.

Charlene started thumping at Lou's arms and back, trying to revive him, I suppose, while tears streamed down her face and she repeated, "No, no, no!"

Well, when someone goes down in the field, it pays to have an RN on hand. Ever the nurse, Sue leapt up and raced to Lou, though I knew it was useless. Checking his pulse, trying to stop the convulsions. It was a noble effort. When I go down for the count, I sure hope Sue is around.

She made a few attempts to resuscitate Lou on the spot, but couldn't get a good angle to help him. Not that there was much she could do. Milton and Quaid got Lou out of the chair and laid him down in the back corner beside the table.

Ranger Rick tried to take charge, ordering people to call 9-1-1, which Astana had already done. The rest just wondered what to do to help.

Sue being Sue, she grabbed some napkins and brushed Lou's nose clean from the dumpling dough that had stuck to it.

Before anyone else did anything, though, I commanded Sue to smell his breath. Out of surprise, everyone obeyed me and stepped back, allowing her to lean over and sniff his breath.

"Marzipan!" she called out. "Yum! Wait - when did he eat marzipan?"

"Almonds," I clarified. "It figures."

At that point, the waitress returned, holding aloft a huge tray with another round of chicken and dumplings. As she saw Lou prone on the floor, her eyes widened, and she dropped the tray of plates.

Crash.

Death. With a side of murder.

As the focus returned to poor Lou, faces turned to me. I wasn't surprised – grief, especially sudden grief, usually seeks someone to blame, however unrelated to the loss itself.

"What are you talking about? Almonds?" Charlene was aghast and afraid.

As she asked, I whipped out my camera and shot a picture of the table scene, despite an offended look from Marsha.

"What are you doing taking photographs?" Marsha demanded. "How incredibly rude!"

"I'm sorry, I just want to be sure we get an accurate documentation of the crime scene before people move things around any more."

Charlene's eyes grew even wider. "Crime scene? What are you talking about?"

Quaid leaned over and patted me on the shoulder. "Yeah, you're taking this a little far, Bertha. Let the poor woman have some space. Her husband's just died. She's in shock. Don't go making this into some drama: the guy just had a heart attack."

I looked up at Quaid and shook my head. "We do not know that. And the longer we hold onto that theory, the harder it is to find the truth. The first minutes are the most sensitive for preserving evidence after a murder. We can't stop Lou from being killed, but we can bring him some justice."

Out of the corner of my eye, I saw Sue nod. Some of the others, though, scooted away from me.

I continued, "After that, we can grieve."

Don't get me wrong. If Lou could be saved, I was all for it. By that point, Astana and the restaurant host had already called for help. Sue had done what she could.

"Killed? What are you talking about, Bertha?" Marsha asked. Everyone was looking at me, suspicious or wary. Everyone except Sue, who knew me well enough by now.

All I had to go on was Sue's prognosis – dead – and the awareness that the suspicious nature of that death would become submerged by the passage of time. I had to think and act fast. If Lou had been killed, it was intended to be done in a way that caused the most confusion possible, and that covered up what had really happened.

Just then, a sound resonated through the room. A low chuckle. We froze.

Funny business.

The chuckle was growing louder with each breath.

It was coming from Olaf. He didn't stop laughing, even as all our eyes turned to him.

Thuy looked at him, sitting next to her. She reached over and shoved him in the arm.

Olaf looked startled, and more awake. The laughter ceased.

Marsha "hmphed" and declared, "It's not funny. A man is dead."

That seemed to remind Charlene of the fact, who started intoning, "No, no no! It can't be! It can't be!"

Suddenly, she rose out of her chair and threw herself onto her late husband's body. She wrapped herself around him and sobbed, his lifeless frame pulsing as she jolted him with every cry. After a moment, Sue kneeled down next to her and patted her back. We all felt her pain. I'm not ashamed to admit that I felt a tear well up.

Finally, the sobs stopped and Charlene came to an upright position. Sue delicately handed her a tissue to wipe her streaming nose. She composed herself and returned to her chair, leaning forward with elbows on her knees.

"How could this happen? He was at the prime of life! We were just – just getting started!"

"Sorry, Charlene," Milton said, as sympathetically as he could. "But he really is dead."

"I'm sorry. It's true," I agreed with a nod. "And I know who killed him."

Setting the scene.

All eyes were on me, again.

"What are you talking about? What happened?" Marsha demanded.

I nodded at her, but instead of answering, I looked around the room, taking in who was where, until my eyes fell on the person I was looking for.

"I'm going to tell you what happened and how. But I want to do this the right way. As Quaid so compassionately pointed out, this might be a particularly traumatic experience for Lou's wife. I just want to warn you, Charlene."

Charlene just shook her head. "It's ok. I want to know what happened. If someone did this to my Lou... I need to know."

Quaid got to his feet, planted his hands on his hips, and shook his head. "Folks, I hate to do this, as Ms. Olson seems to have quite a story in mind for us, but I want to suggest that, as the trip coordinator, we all just take a few deep breaths and rest and wait for the medics to arrive and take over. I know everyone's emotions are up, but maybe we just need a little break."

Rick stood up next to Quaid, a foot shorter but burnished with the fire of someone trying desperately to prove his manhood to an attractive young lady in the room. "Respectfully, Quaid, as the Park Ranger for this tour, I outrank you and I want Bertha – I mean, Ms. Olson – to be able to speak. Please begin, Ms. Olson."

I had to smile at the young man. Hope springs eternal.

First things first, though.

I looked around the room at my audience. Most faces were intent on me, puzzled but curious. Charlene looked in shock, but determined. Marsha was eying Charlene strangely. Milton kept shaking his head, loosened his collar, stared off into the distance. All the others, who'd just met Lou, had gathered in a semi-circle around my chair, seated or standing, giving as much distance to Lou as they could. Quaid was pacing in the doorway, still unconvinced this was a good idea.

And all the while, Lou lay there on the floor beside us. Poor guy. Never knew what was coming at him. I said a quiet prayer for his poor soul.

I gauged that I didn't have much time before the medics and cops arrived, which was for the best. We couldn't leave the guy, but it was also pretty weird sitting around with a corpse in the corner.

"What made you think he was killed?" Marsha asked.

I said, "My nurse friend Sue can offer her professional view, but that was no heart attack."

Marsha squinted at me. "It could have been. He'd had a heart condition, didn't he, Charlene?"

The newly widowed woman nodded.

"But it wasn't a heart attack," Sue agreed with me, then asked, "What was it about the marzipan? Oh wait, I mean, almonds."

I said, "The smell of almonds is a classic sign of poisoning by cyanide."

"Oh, of course..." she said, and I could see the wheels turning in her head, going back through all her nursing school text books for signs and symptoms.

The confused looks on other faces prompted me to continue. Guess not everyone reads as much Agatha Christie as I do. "Cyanide is a potent poison. And the way Lou responded, spasms, convulsions ... all the hallmarks of cyanide poisoning."

"How awful!" Marsha exclaimed.

It was, but I wasn't concerned with that point at the moment. I looked around the circle of faces to find Joyce, half-expecting her to have retreated to the van to escape the chaotic scene in the restaurant. She was seated across the room from the deceased, where she leaned her head back against the wall with eyes closed, breathing deeply. Astana was patting her arm, and Ranger Rick was stationed protectively on her other side.

"Thank you for hanging in here, Joyce," I acknowledged her. "I think you may in fact be very helpful to us."

Marsha was still shaking her head. "I don't get it. Who would kill Lou?"

"Who indeed?" I answered, more mysteriously than she appreciated.

Marsha was looking tense. She kept looking between me and Charlene. For her part, Charlene was just sniffling and staring at her hands, lost in thought or memories of times past. I could guess at what Marsha was thinking – having started my analysis at the same place. It was clear when she asked her next question. "I mean, who would stand to benefit from Lou dying?"

That was indeed always a question to ask. It seemed to bring Charlene back to the present moment. She looked at her friend Marsha, first surprised and then, as realization dawned, offended.

Marsha looked back at her and said defiantly, "I want to know the truth, that's all."

Milton was patting his wife's shoulder and urging her to stay calm.

I had to jump in, before the suspicions and assertions went too far. "I don't think Charlene killed Lou."

Charlene looked, at turns, relieved to have my support and offended that she was under suspicion.

"Of course, it stands to reason that someone might kill because of what they stand to gain. And the wife would gain a good deal by her husband leaving her his wealth. Which, as Charlene herself told you, Marsha, was considerable."

Marsha nodded, brow furrowed.

"How do you know that?" Charlene said to me, aghast.

I shook my head. "Easy to ignore the fat lady in the wheelchair waiting for an open stall in the bathroom, isn't it?"

Charlene *harrumph*-ed. "Well, you can't believe I would kill my Lou for *money*, can you?"

I had definitely wondered that very thing, and her friend Marsha seemed to have as well. Taking the accusation on myself, I answered, "I don't know you, so I *don't* know if you could do such a thing. But I don't think you were Lou's killer. Someone else was, however. You had motive, Charlene. But you also would have plenty of other opportunities – likely better opportunities than this one – to get away with a murder. This trip would give you cover, but also increase the risk."

Sue jumped in, "Unless someone wanted to frame her for murder! How awful!"

"That is, of course, one possible motive. But you see, there is also the possibility that someone was motivated to kill by what they would gain simply by seeing Lou lose his life. Someone with enough history with the man that he just wanted to watch Lou die."

Charlene sobbed. And I saw out of the corner of my eye Thuy punch Olaf in the arm again, just as he was about to launch into another round of ill-timed laughter.

Play by play.

"We'll get to the motive in a minute. First, I'd like to lay out how Lou was killed."

"We know how he died: cyanide," Sue said. "Wait – how did he ingest cyanide?"

Ranger Rick had apparently not lost his appetite and was finishing up his meal as we talked. But at this point he gently placed down the bite he had between greasy fingers. He swallowed, then asked, "Was it in the dumplings?"

I resisted rolling my eyes. "No, Rick. Not the dumplings. Not the chicken, either. Go ahead and finish your dinner."

Marsha's eyes were boring into mine. I could see the wheels spinning, her years of schoolteacher training piecing together how the unruly class clowns had pulled off their latest prank. "Maybe it was in the pills."

I nodded.

Marsha turned to Charlene again, the accusation evident without a word. Thankfully, Charlene was too stunned to notice. Her mouth was agape, eyes wide.

"No, no, no! But *I* gave him his pills!" she sputtered. "Are you saying... I handed him... poison? That can't be!"

"I'm sorry to say it, but you may have."

"You should probably go wash your hands," Sue pointed out, and she wasn't wrong.

But I was not to be deterred from my narrative. "Charlene, you were sure having a lot of trouble reading that menu. And picking out the right pills. At first, I wondered if you were having a stroke. Then, I wondered if you had been faking it, trying to draw attention to not being able to keep track of details like that."

I was thinking of how annoyed I'd been at her simpering tone. It had been suspicious, but not how I'd thought. "Finally, I realized that was just how you always talked to people. And you really couldn't see the words."

"Of course not," Charlene said, warily.

"I think someone planted the poison in Lou's pill box, for this very meal. So that you would hand him the poison, here at this restaurant, without knowing what you were doing."

Marsha was no less suspicious. "But if someone were trying to kill Lou with poisoned pills, how could they risk it putting them in his pill box, and counting on Charlene to not notice what she was handing him? I know exactly what my and Milt's pills and vitamins look like. I would notice if someone stuck extra pills in there."

I'd thought through Marsha's points already, and appreciated her quick thinking. (Even if I was, after all, quicker.) She was on the right path, she just hadn't put the pieces together yet. "You might <u>not</u> notice if you didn't have your reading glasses on, though, would you? None of us would. A small white tab, mixed in with the rest of the noontime pills? Easily missed if you couldn't focus on what you were handling."

"Charlene was wearing her reading glasses," Marsha pointed out.

"She was wearing reading glasses," I explained. "But not *her own* reading glasses."

Charlene gawked, then picked up the glasses she'd had on, squinting at them to figure out what was going on.

I turned to Joyce. "Joyce, thank you for joining us. I think you might be able to help us solve this mystery. Astana, would you mind taking those glasses Joyce was wearing, and seeing if they might be Charlene's? And look and see if the ones Charlene is holding are really Joyce's?"

Astana did as invited, and I was indeed correct. Joyce put on her own glasses and looked relieved – as relieved as she gets, that is.

Now Marsha was looking skeptically at Joyce. Her husband Milton was trying to calm her down and keep her from saying anything, but Marsha had sniffed the scent and was off down the trail. "Why did *Joyce* want to poison Lou?"

Now, Joyce was looking far less relieved. More panicked, in fact. "What? No, I didn't have anything to do with Lou! I didn't... I didn't know Charlene had my glasses... I didn't know!!!"

"Marsha, cool it!" Milton said.

And I chimed in, too. "Marsha, it wasn't Joyce. She was an unwitting participant in this crime."

Sue was smiling at me – proud of her old friend from Kansas, despite the grave circumstances, it seemed. "How did you figure all that out, Bertha May?"

"Joyce has been fighting headaches this morning, haven't you, Joyce?" She nodded as I continued. "But not at the first falls we visited, right? I realized that she didn't start having the headaches from wearing the wrong glasses until after Bridal Veil Falls. At the Vista House, she couldn't read the historical signs. Bridal Veil was where Lou's killer got back into the van and rummaged through people's things, to try to find Lou's pill box.

"Unfortunately for the killer, the pill box wasn't in the tote bag Lou and Charlene left on the van. Lou didn't carry anything but his wallet. Charlene, however, had her purse on her through the hike – and in the purse were the pill boxes. But the killer did find Charlene's glasses and decided to switch them out, just in case. It was clear that if she didn't need to wear them to see the falls, they were reading glasses, the sort of glasses handy for picking out tiny pills from plastic compartments.

"Joyce just happened to have left her reading glasses on the seat, easily accessible to swap. And since Joyce uses a milder prescription than Charlene wore, the swap left them both having blurred vision."

Everyone was leaning forward in their seats, hanging on my every word. Well, not everyone. Not the killer, I noticed.

And not Olaf, who had dozed off.

Seconds.

Just then, our waitress came back into the room with an update that the Sheriff's deputies were on their way. Sensing the dour mood and eager to serve, she asked if she could get anyone anything. "While you wait," she added.

No one was in the mood for more appetizers, not even Ranger Rick. But Thuy – bless her soul – raised her empty martini glass and clinked the side with her finger nail.

To Marsha's aghast look, Thuy replied with a shrug.

Olaf woke up just then and waved at the waitress. "Me, too."

Honestly, they weren't the only ones who could use a drink.

As the waitress left to mix some cocktails, Marsha got us back on track. "Bertha, you still haven't explained how the killer got the poison into Lou's pill box. If they couldn't do it on the van, when did it happen?"

"Yes, that part did not work according to their plan. So the killer had to think fast and retool, and make the most of a rather unusual prop to make the scheme work out. The killer placed the cyanide in Lou's pill box right here, at the table. And no, it wasn't sleight of hand. The trick was a little less subtle.

"About six and a half... maybe seven feet tall, in fact."

Sue bolted upright, her eyes wide. "The Chicken Man!"

Rick gasped and Milton scratched his chin and Quaid shook his head.

I nodded. "It was the Chicken Man, alright."

Milton remained confused. "Quaid in the chicken costume put poison in the pill box? How?"

Marsha attempted a different theory. "You're saying that Quaid was dressed as a chicken to be a distraction while the killer put the poison in the pill box. So that we weren't paying attention. Was Quaid in on it, then?"

I replied, "You're right that Chicken Man was a distraction for us. To get us out of the dining room and onto the deck for that photograph, far from where the killer was placing poison into Lou's pill compartment."

Ranger Rick was squinting and rubbing his temples. He turned toward Quaid. "You told me about wearing the chicken costume to surprise everyone here – were you planning all along for this? I thought it was just one of the jokes you always like to pull on these trips."

I raised one dramatic eyebrow. "But who was in the chicken costume, really? Do we *know* that it was Quaid?"

"Who else would it be?" Sue asked. And I hated to tell her the answer.

I didn't have to. Joyce said, "I heard Quaid talking to the bus driver about wearing it. I didn't know he meant a chicken costume, but he was getting him to do something to entertain us during dinner. He didn't want to, but Quaid was persistent."

Rick was incensed. "Eduardo did that? We've contracted with Capitol Micro-Bus Lines for years! I can't believe he took part in this! That's outrageous! We'll have their license..."

"Cool it, Rick," I urged. "I suspect he didn't know what was happening. Probably didn't know anything about the poison – just assumed Quaid didn't want to wear the costume. Is that your impression, Joyce?"

She nodded.

I hoped the killer was realizing that it didn't pay to overlook anybody – people understand a lot more than the world gives them credit for.

Sue was looking troubled, though. "But if it was the bus driver – this man Eduardo – who was in the chicken costume... then where was Quaid that whole time we were out taking the picture?"

I looked at Sue sadly. She already knew the answer.

Chicken Man.

Quaid had seemed distracted, but had clearly been listening. "I don't know about all this, this whole story you're giving us, Bertha. Why are you so sure of Charlene's innocence? She stood to gain the most from Lou's death. I mean, if this *was* a murder – which I'm not convinced about, you know – then isn't it usually the wife who does it?"

"Not so worried about troubling a new widow, are we, now?" I challenged Moorhouse. With good reason.

Marsha jumped in, now coming to her friend's defense. "You need to leave poor Charlene alone, Quaid. Have some respect. We can all see it now – see through that stupid chicken costume and everything. It was you who poisoned poor Lou! And you wanted to pin it all on Charlene, too. Thank goodness Bertha was here to catch you, you rotten murderer, you!"

Sue was shaking her head. "Quaid killed Lou. How terrible!"

"Yep, there you have it. The means, the opportunity, the man. Quaid Moorhouse, with the cyanide – and the chicken costume – in the roadhouse diner. With a side of dumplings."

I turned my head to face Quaid, who was sweating and red but still trying to smile like it was all a joke.

I asked, "What I don't understand, however, is the motive. Why did you do it, Quaid? *Why* did you kill Lou?"

The man just stammered, then buckled down on his denial. "I don't have any reason to hurt Lou. Charlene would, or maybe his friends – I don't know. But I just met the man. Of course I wouldn't have any reason to kill him."

Milton cleared his throat. "Excuse me, but actually, I might be able to answer that question for you, Bertha."

This was the final piece in the puzzle. And Milton didn't disappoint.

"A name like Quaid Moorhouse is one you don't easily forget. Even if he changes his hair, beard, clothes."

"Or pretends to put on a chicken costume," Sue added. It seemed that her affection had cooled off, now that she knew the guy was a killer. She didn't appreciate being part of his murderous scheme.

"I thought I recognized the name as soon as Quaid introduced himself at the start of the trip," Milton explained. "I tried to ask Lou about it, but he brushed me aside. Then I put it together. I do Lou's taxes, you know. Used to be an accountant, you see. And one of the files Lou had me looking through were expenses related to a lawsuit, filed by a bunch of Pendleton farmers and ranchers who'd been forced to foreclose on their land, back right after the crash of '08. They'd gotten together to sue Lou and his real estate trust for some shady business practices related to the sales and some high-interest loans in the preceding years. Nasty stuff, if it was true."

Charlene was glaring at him. Milton coughed.

"Anyway, I don't like to speak ill of the dead. It was still being decided in court, though I don't think the ranchers had any chance of winning, however much pressure they'd been under to sell – it was all within the letter of the law. Just not very nice. Anyway, Moorhouse was one of the ranchers on that lawsuit, a dispossessed heir."

There we had it. Motive as well as means and opportunity. It was just time for the cops to come in and we could shout, "Cuff 'im."

"I just wish I'd put it together sooner," Milton was shaking his head. "I had no idea..."

"Don't beat yourself up. How could you know Quaid would be so bitter he would kill?" I reassured the man.

Ranger Rick was appalled in a different direction. "You asked me to switch tours, just so you could come on this trip because Lou would be here? You'd been planning all this, Quaid? And you dragged the parks department into it? How could you?"

Moorhouse seemed to realize the jig was up. His eyes wide, head shaking. Then he turned and bolted out the doorway.

Unluckily for him, his exit was blocked.

By a seven-foot tall chicken.

Motivation.

His unwitting accomplice, the bus driver Eduardo, was not interested in catching any rap for Moorhouse's antics, and he pinned the man in his preternaturally large wings, to await the police. And within minutes, there they were – three Multnomah County Sheriff's deputies for Moorhouse, and a flank of paramedics for Lou. Even if he couldn't really use their services by that point.

"Quaid, how could you?" Sue asked him. "Why did you do it? Why did you kill off Lou?"

Moorhouse was defeated. "Your friend got it right. And that Milton, too. Yes, I was mad at him about the land. Of course I was. The nasty snake – stole people's homeland out from underneath their feet. He got my uncle's land, just a few years after I'd moved out there. Plenty of us got fleeced by Lou. My uncle had been there for generations. It was where my mother grew up. I would've inherited that whole ranch – but then Lou moved in like a snake, just to make a quick buck off our hardship. Offered loans he knew we couldn't pay, sky-high interest rates, then foreclosed on the land, made money hand over fist off our misfortune.

"You should've seen me, hopping mad, that day he drove up in his shiny car with the contract to buy my uncle out to settle the debt. What he thought that land was worth. A skunk. A devil, that's what he was! I would've been happy to kill him right then and there.

"The only thing holding me back was Felicia. Beautiful woman, real salt of the earth. I'd never want to hurt that woman – however much of a snake her husband was. But then, he up and quits her, too, leaves her alone back home to run off with this new lady. 'Course, I only heard about that through the grapevine. I'd already had to leave the land, move out to the city. And then I see his name on the list, registered for this trip. It was the perfect chance to get back at him for everything he'd done to us. Who'd miss the old codger, anyway?" Quaid was fuming. "Serves him right. He made a killing off us. Drove my old friends to the bottle or pills, a string of overdoses and suicides. What's Lou's life worth after that?"

He'd said his piece, and it was time for Quaid Moorhouse to end the day's saga in the back seat of a police car.

As they pulled away, Lou's body was being zipped into a bag, with a tearful Charlene holding the hand of her beloved husband's corpse for every last moment they'd let her. He was lifted onto a gurney and rolled outside, Charlene following all the way. Swirling with emotions, Marsha and Milton walked beside their friend. They joined her in the deputy's car, Marsha's comforting arm around the widow's shoulder.

Some of Tad's waitstaff had filtered into the room, sighing and shaking their heads at the task of clean-up before them.

As for our part, we said our goodbyes to Tad's roadhouse diner. Thuy chugged the last of her martini, and we filtered outside to the van in the parking lot.

Ranger Rick, clearly out of his depth, attempted to resume command of the situation. Surveying our downtrodden faces, he clapped his hands together. "Who's up for some Burgerville?"

It wasn't the worst idea in the world, so we piled back in for the Elderwagon's first trip through a drive-thru burger restaurant.

As we looked out the window at the Columbia River, the sun was starting to slide toward the western horizon, lighting the hillsides and houses with a new, almost urgent glow. Sue was finally taking in the scenery.

She turned to me and said, "Bertha May, I don't think I'll ever be able to eat dumplings again."

The End.

Acknowledgments.

My gratitude goes out to Jillian D. for the map and delicious cover art, and to Rita D. and Rhonda J. for editorial comments.

My gratitude goes also to the beautiful lands of the Pacific Northwest, that inspire any visitor or resident, especially the waterfalls of the Columbia River Gorge that are part of the territorial lands of the Cowlitz, Cascades, and Confederated Tribes of Grand Ronde.

Don't miss out!

Visit the website below and you can sign up to receive emails whenever A. Zed publishes a new book. There's no charge and no obligation.

https://books2read.com/r/B-A-YKJO-DYYNB

BOOKS 2 READ

Connecting independent readers to independent writers.

Also by A. Zed

Chicken 'n Dumplins 'n Death
Happy Holidays

About the Author

A. Zed is an enthusiastic vegetarian living in Portland, Oregon. As a child of a librarian, the author was raised to love books and currently frequents the Holgate, Mid-county and Belmont branches of the Multnomah County Library.